When the Elephant Walks

When the

Keiko Kasza

G.P. Putnam's Sons   New York

Elephant Walks

Copyright © 1990 by Keiko Kasza
All rights reserved. This book, or parts thereof,
may not be reproduced in any form without permission
in writing from the publishers.
Published simultaneously in Canada
Printed in Hong Kong by South China Printing Co. (1988) Ltd
Designed by Christy Hale

1 2 3 4 5 6 7 8 9 10

Library of Congress Cataloging-in-Publication Data
Kasza, Keiko. When the elephant walks / Keiko Kasza.
p.   cm.   Summary: When the Elephant walks he
scares the Bear who runs away and scares the Crocodile
who runs away and scares the Wild Hog in this never-
ending animal story.
[1. Animals—Fiction.] I. Title.
PZ7.K15645Wh   1990 [E]—dc19   88-26748 CIP AC

ISBN   0-399-21755-X

To Alexander Taisuke Kasza

When the Elephant walks…

he scares the Bear.

When the Bear runs away...

he scares the Crocodile.

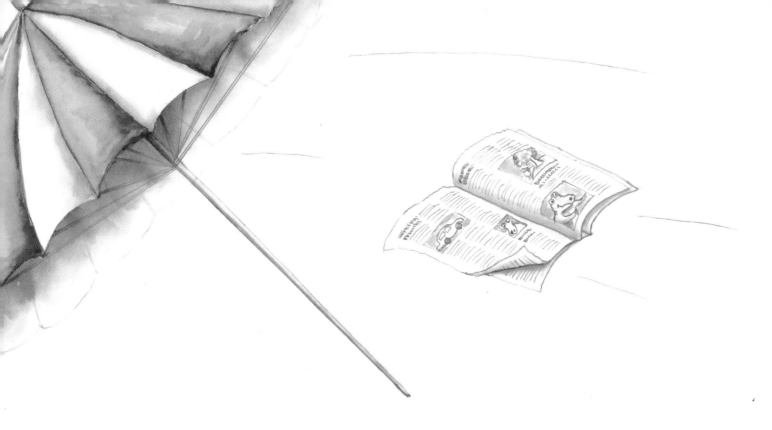

When the Crocodile swims for his life…

he scares the Wild Hog.

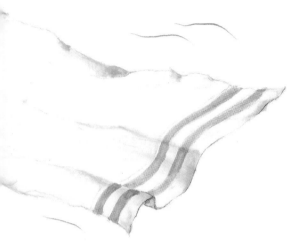

When the Wild Hog dashes for safety…

he scares Mrs. Raccoon.

When Mrs. Raccoon
flees with her baby…

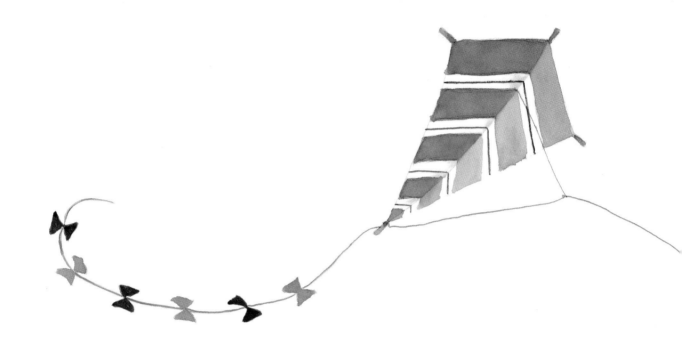

they scare the little Mouse.

But when the little Mouse
scurries in terror...
...Well, who would be scared
by a little Mouse?

E
Kasza, Keiko.
  When the elephant walks

1-3

	DATE DUE		